Mu
Cockington Court

Ken Mackenzie

Old Mate Media

Book and Cover design by Old Mate Media

Edited by Professor Simon Truscott

All enquiries to: books@oldmatemedia.com

Published by Old Mate Media

Paperback ISBN: 978-1-925638-87-5

Digital ISBN: 978-1-925638-88-2

oldmatemedia.com

Contents

To my mum who passed away in 2020.
A special lady who believed I could do anything, my mum.

Chapter 1

It was just after eleven in the morning. In the small thatched cottage village of Cockington, nestling in the Chelston valley, in the heart of the Devonshire countryside, the village was quiet and peaceful, and just waking up.

The village centre comprised one small village shop, which also housed the local post office and chemist. Directly opposite is the Old Forge, a thatched open workshop where the locals would meet and chat, while the farrier shoed their horses.

Following the path from the forge around the back of Mill cottage is Lanscombe House, complete with a working water wheel. The long lane would then bring you to the Manor House. A grand imposing house fit for the lord of the manor, the Cockington family, long since departed.

Inspector Findlay until now had never had cause to visit the Manor. It had been left unattended and almost forgotten for over three decades, although the villagers did occasionally do their best to maintain it and its grounds. The great hall was the same as the day Sir David Cockington died. Sir David was the last of the Cockington family, and they had sat in residence for over two hundred years.

Findlay entered the great hall. He simply stood and stared at the sight in front of him. A hall as big as the village green with arched windows running down both sides ceiling to floor, and covered with years of dust and grime. At the other end of the great hall was the largest mirror he had ever seen. It filled the entire wall, surrounded by its ornate gold frame.

Findlay glanced over to the corner where he could see the outline of a man standing, head bowed and cap in hand. Findlay began walking towards him, every footstep echoed around the room like the precision of a beating drum.

Findlay couldn't help but notice the smell of must and damp in the air, and although it was bright sunshine, there was a distinctive chill that filled the whole room.

"Dan," said Findlay.

"I had no idea it was you, sir," said Dan. "I was cutting back some trees. I just happened to look in the window. I sent word to get you straight away."

Dan owned Molt's farm at the top of Cockington lane, four generations of his family had worked the Cockington land. Dan had never married, so he would probably be the last.

"I believe you have something to show me?"

"It's this way sir," said Dan.

The two men walked into the entrance hall to the manor. It had a sweeping marble staircase which divided at the top into two hallways. "That's just as I found him, sir," said Dan, "just hanging there."

After 25 years on the force, Findlay had never got used to what appeared to be a suicide, but that sick feeling in the bottom of his stomach never got any easier.

"Right Dan," said Findlay, "I can manage from here, I know where to find you."

"Yes sir, of course. I'll be on my way. "

"Oh, Dan?" said Findlay, "keep this to yourself for now, I don't want half the village turning up for a look."

Dan nodded and left.

Findlay wasn't your usual detective. No trilby hat or crumpled raincoat. He was old school, slight of build, always smartly dressed and wouldn't dream of leaving the house without a clean shirt and a smart tie. His wife Margaret made sure of that.

He walked around the hanging remains of a man. The body had been there some time, he thought to himself. Whoever he was, he didn't want to fail. He had tied his feet together so he couldn't reach out to pull back the chair that he used for his final leap. 'Why here? Why Cockington Court?' thought Findlay. 'The Court is surrounded by trees, why break in here to do it?'

The rope had been tied to a rail some three metres up at the top of a staircase. Findlay was staring at the rope and couldn't help thinking, 'if you're going to hang yourself, why jump from a chair? It would be a slow, painful strangulation. Why not just jump from the top?

"Instant." He whispered to himself.

Just then, the door from the hall opened and Sergeant Todd entered. "Morning Sir," he said.

"Morning Sergeant."

"Oh dear", said Sergeant Todd, taking out a handkerchief and holding it to his nose. "He's been there a day or two sir. He's a bit ripe!"

Sergeant Allan Todd, in his late twenties; a most likeable young man, maybe not the quickest, but what he lacked in speed he made up for in other ways, or as Mrs Findlay would say, a very nice young man.

"Yes," said Findlay, "been there a couple of days at least."

"Tell me Sergeant, does anything look strange to you?"

"Strange sir?" Said Sergeant Todd. "In what way?"

"I'm not sure," said Findlay, "it's just a feeling."

"Tell me, Sergeant, if you were going to hang yourself, would you spend time tying your feet together? Surely it's a quicker way to go if you fall from a height rather than jump from a chair?"

"Can't say I have ever had cause to think about it, sir. I suppose so," replied Sergeant Todd. "Either way it wouldn't hurt for long."

Findlay stood for a moment, twisting the winder on his watch. Something he had a habit of doing when he was deep in thought.

He bent forward and stared at the victim's feet. "Do we know what this unfortunate fellow did for a living Sergeant?"

Sergeant Todd thumbed through the notebook he was holding. "Err... seems he worked at Jackson sawmill sir."

"The rope around his feet," said Findlay, "look at the knot."

Sergeant Todd looked inquisitively at the rope. He shook his head slowly. "Sorry Inspector, I'm not sure what you mean."

"The knot, it's an old-style Fisherman's knot. It's called a cleat. Why not just tie a straightforward knot?"

Sergeant Todd shook his head. "Can't say I would have noticed, sir. Does it make a difference? He's still dead."

"Maybe Sergeant...maybe."

"Has the photographer arrived?"

"Yes sir, he's outside."

"Make sure he gets pictures of the feet. Especially the knot." Said Findlay.

"Do we know who he was?"

"Yes sir, his name was Steve Gregson. 34 years old, single, well known in the village. No previous but known to dabble in the odd box from the back of a lorry. Doesn't seem to of had a girlfriend, but he did see the barmaid from the Drum Inn occasionally."

"Right Sergeant," said Findlay, "next stop the Drum."

"Excellent," whispered Todd.

Findlay glared at him over the top of his black-rimmed glasses. A look the sergeant had become used to.

They made their way down the hill into the village.

Chapter 2

A cosy countryside establishment that had stood as the only pub for over two hundred years, the Drum was dimly lit with an open roaring log fire that glinted off the horse brasses adorning every wall, and the smell of burning logs filled the air.

The two men made their way to the bar. "Quiet," remarked Sergeant Todd.

"I wouldn't really know," said Findlay, "Mrs. Findlay and I don't drink."

"No sir of course not."

"Yes gentlemen, what can I get you?" It was Sally. She had worked behind the bar of the Drum Inn for almost five years. An attractive girl. Tall and slim, with jet black hair that she always wore in a tight ponytail. Sally was well-liked by just about everyone that frequented the pub, except of course, for their wives.

"Good evening," said Findlay abruptly. "I'm DCI Findlay and this is Sergeant Todd. We are from…"

"I know who you are Inspector," said Sally, "and I know Sergeant Todd. Don't I Sergeant?"

Todd's face turned a crimson red. "Yes, Sally, you do," said Sergeant Todd. "I've popped in here from time to time, sir."

"Yes, so you have Allan!" said Sally with a grin.

Findlay looked over his glasses and raised his eyebrows. "Really Sergeant," he said.

"So what can I do for you Inspector?" said Sally.

"I believe you know of a Stephen Gregson?"

"Yes," said Sally, "why do you ask?"

"What was your relationship with him?"

Sally bit her bottom lip, and said, "Don't really have one Inspector. He isn't the relationship type. Truth be known Inspector, he's a bit of a pig."

Findlay raised his eyebrows and stared over his glasses at Sally. "Not a lot of love lost then?" said Findlay.

"You could say that, yes," she said. "He's been messing me around for months."

Over an hour I waited for him last night, stood me up he did. "

Findlay slowly turned. He looked at Sergeant Todd, then turned back to Sally.

"I have some bad news I'm afraid," said Findlay, "the body of Stephen Gregson was found this afternoon at Cockington Court."

"He's dead!" gasped Sally.

"I'm afraid so," said Findlay. "Tell me Sally, when did you hear from him last?"

She stood silently for a few seconds, taking in what Findlay had just said.

"Like I said Inspector, he was supposed to have met me last night."

"He called in for a drink around one. Was he alone?" said Sergeant Todd.

"Yes, I think so. It was quite busy, but I'm sure he was on his own. Oh my god, how did he die?" asked Sally.

"We aren't sure yet," said Todd. "It looks like suicide."

Inspector Findlay glared at him, "I think you've said enough Sergeant, don't you?"

"Yes sir. Sorry."

"So, Sally," said Findlay, "did you see him leave at lunchtime?"

"Not really," she replied, "as I said, we were very busy."

Just then, the squeaky old door to the bar opened and slammed shut with a bang.

Findlay and Sergeant Todd looked around. It was none other than Tom Lipman, the Lord Mayor of Torquay, the nearby town, and a Cockington resident.

"Well, well," said Lipman, "if it isn't Detective Inspector Findlay and his sidekick, Sergeant Nod!"

"No sir, that's Todd, not Nod."

"He knows that sergeant," said Findlay.

"Not like you to frequent our local hostelry Inspector, although your sergeant is one of our regulars. Isn't that right Sergeant?"

Findlay again gave his sergeant another look of disapproval.

"So what brings you in here Inspector?"

Immediately Sally blurted out, "it's Steve Gregson, he's dead."

"Really?" said Lipman. "Forgive me if I don't seem surprised."

"Well yes, you don't look very surprised actually," remarked Sergeant Todd.

"I'm not," said Lipman. "It was only a matter of time before he upset the wrong people."

"What does that mean?" asked Findlay.

"Well," said Lipman, "he did have an eye for the ladies, especially the married ones. Plus he did mix with some unsavoury types."

"And how do you know all this?" asked Findlay.

"It's a small place Inspector, not a lot goes on I don't get to hear about as Mayor."

"So, Inspector, any clues yet as to who did it?"

"Not yet," replied Findlay. "I wasn't aware I said anyone else was involved?"

"Well no," said Lipman, "I just presumed."

"Well, don't presume!" Snapped Findlay.

"Anyway, I'm sure you will hear about any developments before I do."

Lipman smiled. "I dare say I will Inspector. I dare say."

"Very well Sally, that will do for now. If you remember anything else about last night, be sure to tell myself or Sergeant Todd. I'm sure he will be, 'popping in' at some point. Isn't that right Sergeant?"

"Don't forget I'm opening the village fete this afternoon," said Lipman. "I presume you and your lady wife will be attending?"

"Highly unlikely," said Findlay, "being in the same village as you is enough for me."

Lipman grinned. "Now, now, Inspector, let's not get personal."

Findlay glared at him for a few seconds, which to Sergeant Todd seemed like hours.

"Sergeant!" said Findlay in a loud voice, "time we left."

The two men turned and walked towards the door. Suddenly Findlay stopped, he turned around and with a grin he said. "Actually Mr Mayor, I will be at the village fete…"

Mayor Lipman was no longer smiling. "Whatever makes you happy Inspector."

The pub door slammed behind them. They stood for a moment on the front step. Findlay slowly buttoned up his coat.

Sergeant Todd looked at him. "So you're going to the fete opening sir?"

"Of course not Sergeant, but did you see Lipman's face? He will spend the whole afternoon looking out for me!" Findlay smiled. "Just a little white lie Sergeant."

They began their walk back up the hill towards Findlay's office. Not much was being said until Sergeant Todd suddenly stood still. "Why do you dislike Mayor Lipman so much, sir?"

Findlay glared at him.

"I'm sorry sir, I've been with you for over seven years, and in all that time I've never heard you say anything positive about him."

Findlay looked his Sergeant in the eye. "Very well," he said, "over there."

They walked over to a wooden seat just off Cockington lane and sat down.

The pair sat for a few moments saying nothing. They just stared down into the valley and out towards the sea.

"Beautiful here," said Findlay.

"It is sir, yes."

Findlay cleared his throat. "What I'm about to tell you Sergeant…it can't go any further, do you understand?"

"Yes sir, of course," said Todd quietly.

Findlay unbuttoned his jacket, folded it neatly and laid it across his knee. He sat bolt upright.

"When I first arrived in Torquay, over thirty years ago, I was very new. I was a young man looking to make an impression, especially on the local mayor, him being my boss."

"He invited Mrs Findlay and I to the annual Christmas ball at Oldway Mansion in Paignton. Mrs Findlay was so looking forward to going. She picked out her ball gown and arranged to go into town to have her hair done."

"The night before the ball, I called into Torquay town hall to see Lipman, just to say thank you for the invitation and tickets. It meant a lot to Mrs Findlay and I."

"I got to his office door and overheard voices. It was the Mayor and Dan Conner. Conner owned the old stable yards in Cockington, he was selling the yards to a Plymouth building company, and they wanted to build houses on them. They were both laughing. Conner was going to pocket thousands, but there's no planning permission to build on that land, unless the Mayor granted it, of course."

"Conner was counting out a pile of cash, the Mayor's share of the deception, plus our illustrious Mayor would have made some more money selling the building rights as well. I walked in on them, and they knew I had heard everything. Both Lipman and Conner threatened to ruin my career on the force, or worse, if I ever talked about what I had heard."

Sergeant Todd had sat motionless, listening as Inspector Findlay opening himself up for the first time to his friend and colleague.

"So what happened," asked Todd.

"Nothing," said Findlay in a quiet voice. "I had just found out that the Mayor was corrupt and he had the power to destroy me. I walked out and never mentioned it again."

"So that's why you and the Mayor hate each other?"

"Hate is a strong word Sergeant. Let's just say, we only speak when we have to."

"So, did you get to the Christmas ball?" asked Todd.

"No Sergeant, we did not. Even now, after all these years, I can still see the disappointment on Mrs Findlay's face. In thirty years, we have never attended the annual Christmas ball. Not once."

Sergeant Todd sat quietly and said nothing.

Findlay suddenly stood up. "Right Sergeant, I've changed my mind! Let's get to this village fete."

Chapter 3

They both walked slowly back up the hill towards Fletcher Farm. The village fete had been held at the farm, on the same date every year for generations. It was known locally as 'the apple pie fair', and dated back to the thirteenth century. People from all around the Torquay area would arrive to spend the day apple picking from the Cockington orchards. The villagers would set out their stalls selling local wool and knitted items produced in the many thatched cottages around the village. Homemade cakes and pies were always popular, and of course, thick hot apple pies.

It wasn't long before Inspector Findlay and Todd arrived. They reached the wooden farm gate to the field." Morning inspector, morning Sergeant Todd. How be yee both?" It was Danny Fletcher. His family had farmed the land around Cockington for seven generations.

"We are fine Dan," said Findlay. "Have you seen Mayor Lipman?"

"Unfortunately, yes," said Dan. "He's over at the beer tent I think."

"Thank you," replied Findlay with a smile.

"Todd," said Findlay, "no free drinks, no free food. Is that understood?"

"Of course, sir," replied Todd, looking quite put out at the fact he wasn't going to get any free food or drink.

"We don't want people thinking we are dishonest, do we?"

"No sir," replied Todd, "of course not."

At that, Findlay turned and walked towards the beer tent. As he got closer, he could see a sign hanging outside the tent, it was fixed to an old apple tree, 'Drum 2' it read, which made Findlay smile.

He drew level with the doorway and instantly saw Lipman sitting in a corner holding a glass of cider. He was talking with two men Findlay had never seen before. Findlay was tempted to go in just to annoy Lipman but thought better of it. He decided to have a look around.

Meanwhile, Sergeant Todd had gone for a look at the assortment of stalls.

"See anything you fancy?" said a familiar voice.

Todd swung around. "Sally," he said awkwardly. "Hello, how are you? Imagine bumping into you here."

Sally smiled and shook her head, "yes," she said. "How unusual to find me behind the bar pulling pints at the village fete, considering I work in the pub that is!"

"Sergeant Allan Todd," she said playfully, "I do believe you are blushing."

"Don't be ridiculous," he replied, blushing. He laughed and started to walk away.

"Wait!" shouted Sally. "Allan, wait! Please, I'm sorry. I didn't mean to embarrass you."

"You didn't," he snapped back.

"Let me buy you a beer, just to say sorry."

"I'm on duty," he said, "and I'm under strict orders; no food or drink."

"So what exactly are you looking for?" said Sally.

Todd stood for a moment in deep thought. "Do you know Sal? I have no idea. The inspector didn't say."

"So how about that beer?"

"Yes, why not?" he said. "One won't hurt, will it?"

Sally put her arm through his and they made their way to the beer tent in the middle of the fete.

They had barely entered when Mayor Lipman made his way over to their table.

"Sergeant Todd," said Lipman, "and the lovely Sally, I do hope you're not thinking of having a pint sergeant? You being on duty and all!"

Todd remained seated. He placed his hands flat on the table top and looked up at Lipman. He did not have to speak, his look was enough.

Lipman smiled. "Give us a moment Sally," said Lipman.

Sergeant Todd spoke out without a second thought. "You stay where you are Sally."

Lipman glared at her. "Not if she wants to keep her job she won't."

Sally looked at him with anger, but she knew what he was like. "I'll be back shortly Allan," she said and left.

Lipman sat down.

"Make yourself at home," said Todd.

Lipman stared at him for a few seconds then said, "It must be difficult."

Sergeant Todd looked at him. "Difficult?" he replied. " What are you talking about?"

"We both know you continually cover for Findlay."

"What?" said Todd.

"He's getting close to retirement. It won't be long before he's thinking about hanging his raincoat up. You could take his place, sergeant, or should I say, Inspector Todd? A word in the right ear could make that happen."

Todd glared at him, "and what's in it for you?"

"Oh," said Lipman, "just the odd favour now and then. "

"Really!" said Todd. "Like what?"

"I don't know Sergeant. Maybe now and again you could turn a blind eye."

Todd sat for a moment, then said. "A blind eye? You mean ignore illegal goings-on."

"Just now and then Sergeant. Here and there. "

Todd sat for a few seconds then said. "You really are a treacherous little man aren't you? Inspector Findlay was right about you!"

Lipman glared at him. "You do yourself no favours making an enemy out of me."

Todd said nothing. He stood up and left.

He hadn't gone far when he heard Sally shouting at him. "Allan wait!"

He was suddenly in no mood for village fetes.

"So what did Lipman want?" she asked.

"What he always wants," said Todd.

"Oh," said Sally. "I didn't think he was up to any good."

"Can you believe he actually tried to bribe me?"

"He's known for being a pig," said Sally. "He's been like that ever since I've known him. The trouble is, he's got influence in high places. He can make life very difficult or very profitable for you."

"I'll not be bribed by the likes of him!" said Todd.

"No," said Sally, "of course not. But sometimes it might pay you to look the other way, especially if it helps your career."

Todd's head spun around. He glared at Sally.

"What's wrong?" she said. "Why are you looking at me like that?"

Todd stared for a few seconds. "I didn't tell you what he wanted Sally. How did you know?"

She stuttered, "You must have."

"No, I didn't. What's going on Sal?" he said.

She looked at him.

He shouted, "what the hell's going on?!"

"I'm sorry Allan. Lipman said if he couldn't convince you it was up to me, he frightens me. He's been talking to strange men over the last couple of weeks, I've no idea who they are, and I don't want to know. Please don't hate me Allan!"

"I don't," he replied, "I'm just disappointed. I thought we were friends."

At that, he stood up and walked away.

"Allan!" she shouted.

He ignored her and kept walking towards the fairground. Sally let him go. She just stood and watched him vanish into the crowd.

Chapter 4

He hadn't gone far when he heard his name being called. Todd spun around to see James Heritage, the local plumber and handyman running towards him.

"Jim!" said Sergeant Todd, "slow down, what on earth is wrong?"

"You have to come quick! I can't find Inspector Findlay anywhere."

"He's at the fair," said Todd, pointing to the fairground field. "What's so important?"

"It's the mill; there's been a terrible accident! You have to come quick!"

The two men made their way across the field towards Scanlon Woods where Todd had left the village's one and only police car.

"Get in," he said to Jim, "this better be good. I spent two hours cleaning this car this morning. I was supposed to drive it to the bandstand where Lipman was going to award the trophy for best apple pie. Then give the winner a ride around the field, sirens an' all. I expect by the time we get up to the mill she will be covered in mud!"

They made their way along the lane towards the sawmill, trying to avoid the many potholes and fallen rocks which littered the lane.

As they pulled into the timber yard, Todd could see a small crowd of workers congregating around one of the storage sheds.

"Make way!" he shouted. "Come on lads, police! Let me through!"

He pushed his way inside. He had seen some sad and some gruesome sights in his time on the force, but nothing could have prepared him for what was in front of him. He stood for a moment, not really knowing what to do. Suddenly, a voice behind eased the tension.

"Come along Sergeant, make way."

It was Inspector Findlay.

"Sir," stuttered Todd, "you're here."

"Once again, Sergeant, your powers of observation astound me. I am here because they called the office. Eddy Doyle came and got me."

Findlay stood with his sergeant and stared at the sight before them.

Findlay slowly walked forward towards the circular saw. A large metal wheel edged with razor-sharp teeth would spin while cutting through the largest of tree trunks.

Findlay stopped just in time and looked down. There on the ground was a large pool of blood which was being soaked up by the sawdust that covered the mill floor. He slowly walked around it and leaned over the machine. On the ground was the body of a man, cut through from shoulder to hip.

Findlay took out his crisp white hanky and held it up to his mouth. "My God," he whispered to himself.

"Sir," said a voice behind him.

Findlay jumped and looked around. "Todd," he said.

"A word to the wise," said Findlay, "if you've just eaten I wouldn't go any further."

Todd, of course, took no notice. He leaned over to see a body lying behind the cutting saw. He slowly straightened up and turned around to face Findlay, ashen-faced and eyes wide open. The two men stared at each other for a few seconds.

Todd being Todd couldn't help himself. "Seems he had a split personality sir."

Findlay raised his eyebrows, "Not funny Sergeant ."

"I know sir, sorry. Just trying to lighten the mood a little."

"I don't think that poor chap would find it amusing."

"No sir," said Todd, "sorry."

"Make sure everyone stays out," said Findlay. "This could be a murder scene, it could be an accident. I hope it's an accident. God forbid anyone would do that on purpose. Where's the mill owner, Jackson?"

"I'll find him," said Todd, and he pushed his way through the crowd of mill workers.

Findlay walked over to where a now large crowd had gathered. "Who found him?" shouted Findlay.

"That be me," said a voice from the crowd. A man stepped forward.

It was George Mallock, a local man. He had worked at Jackson's mill since he was a boy. His family owned most of Torquay at one time, and the family had lived in the village for generations.

"George", said Findlay.

He handed Findlay a plastic sheet. "You might wanna cover him with this," he said.

Findlay reached out and took it.

"How long ago did you find him?" asked Findlay.

George didn't reply, he just stared down at the now mass of congealed red sawdust.

"George. George!" said Findlay in a raised voice.

"I told him nothing good would come of it."

"I don't understand," said Findlay, "told who, what?"

"He was up to no good with them strangers. I told him, it wouldn't end well!"

"I have no idea what you're talking about, George. Come over here and sit. What did you mean? You told him no good would come of it. Come of what?"

"Your dead body. It's Dan, Danny Fletcher."

"What!" said Findlay. "It can't be. We just saw him down at the village fete!"

"Well it is," said George.

"What was he doing up here? He's nothing to do with the mill, he's a farmer."

"All I know," said George, "is that he was angry and scared. I saw him yesterday. He was out cutting the top field getting ready for the fete. I stopped to say hello, he was very quiet, not like him. I've known him all my life Inspector, I knew something wasn't right."

"He didn't tell me everything, but I know it's to do with Scanlon Woods and this timber mill. He said he was meeting an acquaintance of Mr Jackson up here, that's all I know."

"What about Scanlon woods?" said Findlay.

"Dan's family still owns part of the woods. I think Jackson was putting pressure on him to sell. He said he was going to have it out with Jackson, but he goes nowhere these days without those two gorillas flanking him."

Findlay couldn't help but notice George's hands were shaking. "George go home, you've had a shock. Go home, I'll speak with you again tomorrow."

George nodded. He said nothing. He just stood up and walked away.

At that, Sergeant Todd returned. "Jackson's not here sir, they said he's not been in all day."

Findlay slowly nodded. "Very well Sergeant, we will catch up with him later."

A car pulled up at the mill offices. It was Dr Ian Fleming from Torquay hospital.

He walked over to where Findlay and Todd were standing. "Well, well, inspector, never known it so busy. What do we have then?"

"Over here, sir," said Todd, pointing to the circular saw.

Fleming leaned over to have a look. He turned his head and looked at Todd.

"Good heavens!" exclaimed Fleming.

"Very well Sergeant, the transport is on its way to collect this unfortunate, so I won't keep you. Tell the inspector I will let him know my findings as soon as possible."

Todd smiled, still looking at the sheet of plastic on the floor.

"Everything alright?" enquired Fleming.

"Err, yes, sir."

"Right, I'll go then."

Todd came from a very humble background. Talking to doctors, especially a coroner, was a little beyond his comfort zone. He quickly left and soon caught up with Findlay. "The coroner said he could manage and he will be in touch. I left him to it."

They walked slowly back to Todd's police car, now covered in mud and dust from the journey up Scanlon hill. "I thought you said you had cleaned it, sergeant? Isn't that why you finished early yesterday?"

"I did sir, and a good job I made of it!"

Findlay raised an eyebrow and shook his head. "Get in, he said."

They made their way back to the village and soon arrived at the office.

"I'm going home," said Findlay. "I need to sit and think. I can't do that here. I'll see you tomorrow."

"Very good sir, tomorrow it is."

Findlay stood at the gate to his house and just looked at it. He couldn't help thinking how lucky he was. He had a lovely home, a loving wife and a job he loved. He knew it was up to him to go to Dan Fletcher's farm and tell his family the news. He wasn't looking forward to it.

He slowly pushed open the small garden gate and gently closed it behind him.

He took out his keys and opened the front door. He was immediately met with the smell of freshly baked bread and the warmth of the open fire crackling away in what he called the best room. Finlay walked into the kitchen. Mrs F was just filling two large pies with chopped apples.

"Hello dear," said Findlay.

"Oh hello darling," she replied, "I didn't hear you come in."

She took a small towel from the worktop and wiped her hands.

"You're a little earlier today," she said.

"Yes, it's been a long day. I will have to go out again shortly, just for a while."

"Very well dear," she replied, "whatever you say. I bought some lovely apples at the fair, so apple pie for tomorrow."

"Lovely," he said.

Findlay stood for a moment and stared at her. She was small of frame, very slim with shoulder-length auburn hair which had wisps of grey spread about it. He again thought what a lucky man he was.

He made his way to the open fire and stood for a moment staring into the flames while twisting the winder of his watch. Two deaths in a few days, both as yet unexplained. In all his years in Cockington, he had had five deaths, which were eventually all explained. Now two deaths that looked very nasty.

He decided not to sit. He had to get over to Fletcher's farm. It was only right he should be the one to tell Dan's family he wouldn't be coming home.

———⋈———

Chapter 5

The next morning Inspector Findlay was in his office early. He stood looking out onto the village Main Street in deep thought.

The silence was broken as Sergeant Todd arrived. "Morning sir, "he said cheerfully.

"Morning sergeant. Take a seat. Let us see what we have so far."

The two men sat opposite each other. Findlay picked up the file. "Right, what do we have?" as he emptied the file onto his desk.

"We have a possible suicide. One that took the time to tie up his feet. And why do it at the Court? He had obviously been there at least a day."

"Yes Sir," replied Todd, "he was well known around Torquay, and yet nobody missed him for a full twenty-four hours."

"We have a busy pub, where just about everyone in there is either related or knows everyone else. A pub where the barmaid knew him intimately but can't remember if he was alone or not?"

"About that sir," said Todd.

"About what sergeant?"

He told him about his conversation with Lipman, and how he caught Sally out in a lie.

Findlay sat quietly for a moment, all that could be heard was the tick-tock of the old station clock on his wall.

Findlay took a deep breath. "I take it you put him in his place?"

"I did sir, he wasn't happy. I wouldn't put too much blame on Sally, slip of a girl can't stand up against the likes of Lipman."

Findlay picked up the file from his desk. "Right Sergeant, let's carry on. "

"We have our prestigious Mayor who seems to know everything about everyone. So, what does that tell you so far?"

"Err, I'm not sure, sir."

"It tells me that people know more than they are saying, and this was no suicide."

"Today is Friday, pay day. I want you to go down to the Drum. By mid-afternoon, it will be busy with the workers from the mill and the local farms. See what's being said, the news would have spread around by now."

"Oh, and Sergeant? Remember, you're on duty, no alcohol."

"Of course, sir," replied Sergeant Todd.

"I expect you had a few at the fete?"

"No sir, not one."

"I'm impressed," said Findlay, "keep it up!"

"I'm going up to the mill," said Findlay. "Be back at the station by four."

"Yes sir," replied Todd.

The two men parted company. Sergeant Todd didn't need telling twice to go to the pub.

———❌———

Chapter 6

Inspector Findlay climbed into his old silver-grey Volvo, his pride and joy since he bought it 15 years ago when it was new. He made his way slowly up the gravelled tree-lined road that wound its way around the back of Cockington Court and out towards the Jackson sawmill. The journey took around twenty minutes. Anybody else could do it in ten, but he wasn't driving his pride and joy over rough terrain at any kind of speed. Especially the mile or so along the pot-holed road to the mill.

He arrived at the main entrance, parked, and climbed out. He couldn't miss the smell of freshly cut timber. It filled the air like a woodland perfume. It reminded him of his prize roses and how it was nearly time to cut them back, ready for spring. 'I must remember to visit the stables on my way home' he thought to himself, 'pick up a couple of bags of manure.'

He made his way to the glass doors of the main sales office when suddenly the Mill owner, Brian Jackson, appeared at the door. "Inspector!" he said. "To what do I owe this pleasure?"

"I presume you've heard about Gregson?"

"Yes, I have. Dreadful that a young man like that should take his own life, do you know why he did it inspector?"

"We don't know anything as yet, sir. I believe he did some work for you not very long ago?"

"Yes, he did. Just some odd jobs around the offices, painting, etc. I didn't have very much to do with him to be honest, my office dealt with it."

"Was he paid through the books or was it cash in hand?"

"Through the books, inspector, always."

"Then you will have records."

"Of course," replied Jackson.

"I believe it wasn't the first time you had given him work?"

"No, he had done other jobs over the last year or so."

"Did he work alone?" asked Findlay.

"Why all these questions?"

"I'm just trying to get to the bottom of a few things, Mr Jackson."

"May I see your employees' books, wages, etc?"

"And why would you want to see them?"

"Just on the off chance he had anyone helping him. A friend, a work colleague," replied Findlay.

"I'm just on my way home," said Jackson angrily. "It's the weekend."

"I could always get a warrant, sir, " said Findlay. "You could always open up for me on Sunday.""Either is fine for me, although I doubt Mrs Jackson would be very happy with you for ruining her weekend."

Jackson stood for a moment. He didn't want to get on the wrong side of his wife. "Very well," he said. "Please be quick, some of us have homes to go to."

The men made their way up the spiral staircase to the main office. Jackson opened up and made his way to a tall five-drawer filing cabinet. He took out his keys, opened the top drawer, and pulled out a thick black book. He banged it down on top of the desk. A puff of sawdust rose into the air and settled on the piles of paper that were neatly stacked around his office.

Inspector Findlay sat down, brushing the sawdust from his neatly creased trousers. He opened the book and flicked through the pages until he came across the name Gregson.

"It appears our Mr Gregson was a regular visitor," said Findlay.

"Really?" said Jackson, "I wouldn't really know. I have people that deal with pay and staff."

Findlay ran his finger down the list of maintenance work carried out by Gregson.

"Considering he was unskilled labour, he was extremely well paid Mr Jackson. The last entry was on the 18th, last Friday, nearly eight hundred pounds. Just what did he do for you that would earn him eight hundred pounds?"

"There are eleven entries here, totalling almost nine thousand." Findlay lifted his head from the ledger. "Nine thousand pounds? That's a lot of money for a man who just did odd jobs."

Jackson slowly shook his head. "As I said, I have people to do that," replied Jackson, "but I agree it seems like a lot."

Findlay continued thumbing through the pages of the office ledger. He turned to the last page. It was blank, except for one entry, 33D, with the initial L pencilled at the top of the page along with the time 3.00pm.

Findlay made a few notes, sat with both hands planted firmly on the desk and slowly drummed his fingers.

"Very well sir, that will be all for now. I may need to speak with you again."

He stood up and brushed the dust from the seat of his pants.

"Anything I can do to help, Inspector, "said Jackson as he opened the office door.

Inspector Findlay made his way out, climbed back into his car, and drove back to the village. He soon arrived at his office where sergeant Todd was waiting for him.

"Sergeant," he said quietly, "so what news on the local grapevine?"

"It's the talk of the pub sir. Strange thing is, they went very quiet when I walked in. I tried asking a few of the regulars if they had heard anything, they just turned away, seems nobody wants to talk."

"There were a couple of townies…."

"Townies?" asked Findlay.

"Yes sir. People from the city, Plymouth or Exeter, I'm not sure which, but I haven't seen them before. They were talking with Mayor Lipman. I was on my way to their table, but they got up and left. I asked the Mayor who they were. He just said, 'friends', then I came back here."

"Oh, and I only had a lemonade sir."

"I know Sergeant, I can smell it," said Findlay sarcastically.

"It's after five. That will do it for today. Nice and early in the morning, I think it's going to be a long day."

"Yes sir," replied Todd, "bright and early it is."

Sergeant Todd took his coat from the back of the door and left. He made his way down the steep steps from the inspector's office and out into the street. He stood for a moment and buttoned up his coat, raised his collar and started the walk home.

He hadn't gone far when it started to rain." Damn," he muttered. He could see the lights at the pub at the bottom of the hill. 'Well,' he thought to himself, 'I'm on my own time, I don't suppose one will hurt, just till the rain stops.' He picked up the pace as he quickly made his way down the steep hill to the Drum.

He was halfway there when he heard a car engine behind him. He stood back on the steep narrow hill and waited for it to pass. Suddenly, the car veered to the left. It was heading straight for him. He tried to climb the embankment to get out of its way, but it was too late. Thud, it hit him hard, sending him high into the air. He crashed down onto the embankment and rolled down the other side into a field.

He lay very still for a few moments. "There's no pain," he whispered under his breath, "maybe I'm okay."

Suddenly, the heavens opened, and the rain got heavier. He was wet and cold. He tried to roll onto his side and pull himself up. It was then he knew he was in trouble. A searing pain wracked his entire body, a pain he had never before experienced, then blackness.

Chapter 7

The next morning, Inspector Findlay arrived promptly as always at eight. He had his usual cup of tea and read through the morning paper.

Suddenly, the old station clock on his office wall struck nine. He glanced down at his watch and shook his head. "Never on time," he muttered.

There was a knock on his door. "Come in!" he shouted.

The door opened and there stood Mrs Bruce, Sergeant Todd's landlady.

"Mrs Bruce," said Findlay, "what a pleasure! Please come in. What can I do for you?"

"Morning inspector," she said in her usual high pitched Scottish accent. "It's Allan."

"Allan?" repeated Findlay. "Oh, Sergeant Todd," he replied. "I'll have a few words to say to him when I see him. I told him bright and early!"

"That's just it," she interrupted, "he didn't come home last night! He never stays out unless he tells me. I won't cook for him if he isn't coming home."

Findlay rose from his desk. "Strange," he said. "I presumed he was going straight home from here last night."

"Well," said Mrs Bruce, "I waited until gone ten o'clock, he didn't come back."

"Leave it with me," said Findlay. "He's fond of our local pub. Wouldn't surprise me if he had one too many and stayed there last night. I'll go down there now, see what I can find out. Don't you worry my dear, I'm sure he's fine!"

Findlay opened the office door and showed Mrs Bruce down to the street. "I'll let you know as soon as I find him," promised Findlay.

Mrs Bruce made her way home while Findlay climbed into his car and drove down the hill to the Drum Inn.

He pulled up at the front door and looked down at his watch, nine-fifteen. 'The doors didn't open until eleven,' he thought to himself, 'explains why it's so quiet.'

He banged on the oak doors to the pub and waited. He banged again. A top window opened. It was Sally. "Inspector, a bit early, isn't it?"

Findlay looked up and frowned. "Open the door Sally, police business."

Sally made her way down the stairs and opened up. "Come on in," she said.

Findlay stepped inside. He couldn't help but notice the smell of stale beer and cigarettes. He glanced down at the open fire, now nothing but a smouldering pile of ash.

"Well?" said Findlay angrily. "Where is he?!"

"Where's who?" exclaimed Sally.

"My sergeant! Sergeant Todd."

"Why are you asking me? He isn't here."

"I'll ask you one more time Sally, if he's here, please fetch him, he's in enough trouble."

"But he isn't here, I swear!"

Findlay glared at her for a moment. "Did he come here last night?"

"No, it was very quiet. The rain kept most people home I think."

Findlay's concern had now turned to one of worry. It was out of character for his sergeant not to arrive at work. He was usually late, but he always arrived.

"You're sure Sally? He didn't come in here last night?"

"Positive," replied Sally.

"Very well, if you see him tell him I am not happy."

"I will Inspector."

Findlay made his way back up the hill wondering where on earth his sergeant could be? He wasn't the brightest on the force, but Inspector Findlay was quite fond of him.

He made his way to Old Mill cottage where Sergeant Todd had rented a room for the last eight years. By the time he had locked his car, Mrs Bruce was on the doorstep. "Have you found him?" she said falteringly.

"I'm afraid not. I've been to the pub but Sally said she hadn't seen him. Would you know if he was seeing anybody from the village?"

"Not to my knowledge," replied Mrs Bruce.

"Well," said Findlay, "it's all very strange. I'm sure he will turn up. As soon as he does, I'll be sure to let you know."

"Thank you Inspector, I am very worried about him. "

Findlay left and made his way to his car. He wasn't sure if he was angry or concerned. He stood at the side of his car for a moment and stared along the Main Street of the village. He couldn't help thinking, 'why no phone call? Surely if something important had cropped up, he would have let him know.'

He decided to go back to his office half expecting his sergeant to be there, cup of coffee in hand, and a very inventive reason why he didn't get home last night, or more importantly, why he was late for work.

He made his way up the creaking stairwell to his office. As he got closer, he could just make out the shape of a man through the pattern glass standing in his office.

'Todd,' he thought to himself. He angrily thrust open the door. He was about to read the riot act to his sergeant when he realised it wasn't him, it was Lipman the Village Mayor.

"What are you doing in here!?" snapped Findlay.

"The door was open inspector."

Findlay was if nothing else, fastidious. Not locking his door when he went out was something he would never do.

He walked around his desk and sat, folded his arms and said, "How much longer do you have as Mayor?"

"Oh," replied Lipman, "quite a while yet."

"What is it you want?" said Finlay under his breath.

"I believe you paid Paul Jackson's mill a visit yesterday. May I ask what it was you were looking for?"

"NO," replied Findlay.

Lipman walked over to the window and stared down at the street. There were a few seconds of silence, which seemed like an eternity. It was broken by Lipman.

"Mr Jackson is a very important man inspector, a very rich man. He has important friends. You were asking him about Gregson, the man that hung himself."

"And just how would you know that Mr Mayor, unless Jackson had told you?"

"I'm simply saying Inspector. It wouldn't do your career a lot of good if you were to associate the likes of Paul Jackson with anything, shall we say, unsavoury. "

Findlay slowly rose to his feet, both hands on his desk. He glared at Mayor Lipman. "Are you threatening me Mr Mayor?"

"Certainly not Inspector! Let's just say it's a little bit of free advice."

Inspector Findlay was now in a rage. "I've known you for years Lipman. How you became Mayor is beyond me, greased a few palms I've no doubt. Two men are now dead. My job is to find out why and possibly who. I'm well aware of the type of people you do business with. I'm also aware that it's just a matter of time until I come knocking on your door. Now get out of my office!"

Lipman slowly walked over to the door, he turned and said, "You should be very careful what you say Inspector. You and your lovely wife have a good life here. It would be a shame if anything were to happen to spoil that."

Findlay shouted at the top of his voice, "Get out!"

Lipman smiled and slowly closed the door behind him.

Findlay sat in his chair, his hands shaking with anger and his heart thumping in his chest. It took a while for him to regain his composure. He took a deep breath.

'Back to work,' he said to himself, 'now where's that sergeant of mine?'

He was about to collect his coat and continue his search when the phone on his desk rang out.

"Hello? Police," said Findlay.

"Inspector it's Jim Barton over at Mallock farm. You have to come quick!"

"Slow down Jim," said Findlay. "Now slowly, what's wrong?"

Barton continued, "I was feeding the sheep in the top field near Gallows gate. It's Allan Todd, your sergeant, he was laying in the field!"

"What?" exclaimed Findlay. "Is he alright?"

"I don't know Inspector, I called an ambulance, and they took him to Torquay general hospital."

"How long ago was this?"

"Not a half-hour ago," replied the farmer.

Findlay slammed down the phone and grabbed his coat and ran down the stairs.

It wasn't long before he arrived at Torquay hospital.

He hurriedly made his way to the reception desk. "My name is Findlay. You just had an admission from Cockington village?"

"Yes, we did," replied the nurse." Are you family?"

"No," snapped Findlay, "I believe it's my sergeant, Allan Todd."

"And you are?" said the nurse suspiciously.

"I'm Inspector Brian Findlay, Devon and Cornwall Police. Here's my card."

"Very well," she said. "Take a seat. A doctor will be with you shortly."

Findlay walked over to an empty row of seats and sat down. He couldn't help feeling bad about thinking the worst of his sergeant. All the time thinking he was up to no good and there he was laying in a field for god knows how long.

Twenty minutes or more passed when suddenly a door swung open. Findlay jumped to his feet. "Doctor, how is he?"

"You must be Mr Findlay?"

"Inspector Findlay," he replied.

"Well, inspector, he's a very lucky young man. He has a broken collarbone and some nasty cuts and bruises. Considering he spent the night lying in an open field, it could have been a lot worse. "

"Can I see him?"

"Yes," replied the doctor, "just for few minutes. He's in the side ward over there."

Findlay pulled back the plastic curtain. There in front of him was, he had to admit to himself, not just his sergeant, but his friend.

"Well," he said firmly, "this better be good! I was expecting you early this morning." He said with a slight grin, "Oh and I will be docking your pay."

Sergeant Todd told him what had happened. "I don't understand it sir, it was almost as if the car hit me purposely. There was plenty of room, but it came straight at me."

Findlay sat and listened intensely. "Did you get a look at anyone in the car?"

"Not really sir," replied Sergeant Todd, "just a glance at the driver, but only for a second or two."

Findlay couldn't help thinking about what Lipman had said to him, about being careful and not upsetting the wrong people, but surely, not even Lipman would go this far.

"Right Sergeant, seems you're going to be in here for a few days. I'm sure I will manage without you," he said with a smile. "I'll let Mrs Bruce know where you are. I'm sure she will be relieved to know you've turned up."

Findlay made his way back to the village. On the way back, he couldn't stop thinking about Lipman's threat. He decided he would get nowhere going in headfirst. If he was going to get to the bottom of this, he had to be careful. He decided to go home. After today's events, it would be nice to get some peace and quiet.

Findlay sat in his favourite armchair, staring into the open fire. Nothing but unanswered questions going around and around in his head. He could feel his eyes slowly closing. 'Been a hell of a day,' he thought to himself. His eyes closed as he fell into a deep sleep, something he very rarely did.

Chapter 8

He woke with a start; the burning logs in the hearth were now just white ash. He looked at the clock standing on the fireplace above the now dead fire, 2.30am.

Findlay raised himself, better get to bed, he thought. He walked over to pull closed the heavy draped curtains that hung over the lounge window.

He was about to close them when he noticed a dark-coloured car parked in the street opposite his house. "Now who could that be?" he muttered. "I've never seen that car before." He looked around the corner of the lace curtains his wife had hung just the day before. It was difficult to see, but he could just make out the outline of two people. Whoever they were, it was two-thirty in the morning, Findlay being Findlay wanted to know what they were up to.

He closed the curtains and made his way to the front door. He slipped on his heavy winter coat and opened the door. No sooner had he stepped outside that the car engine started and the strange car with its two occupants quickly drove away.

Findlay squinted through the darkness and was able to see the first two letters of the car's registration, DB and a number 7. He quickly made his way back indoors and wrote down DB7, annoyed with himself that he didn't get more.

The next morning, he was in his office at eight. He pulled out the piece of paper with the partial registration. He laid it on the desk and stared at it. If only I had the rest, he thought to himself.

He opened the case file and slid the paper into it. With a sigh, he closed it and pushed it to the end of his desk. Findlay sat for a while. All he could hear was the ticking of the old station clock on his office wall.

He was turning over everything that had happened, trying to make sense of it. "I need help," he muttered to himself. Not something he would admit lightly.

He lifted his old briefcase from under his desk, reached in, and pulled out his diary. He flicked through its pages, not really knowing what he was expecting to see, and stopped.

The page in front of him had the name Bob Newman.

"There's a name I haven't heard in many a year," he said to himself. Sgt Bob Newman, a colleague from the time he spent coming through the ranks. Findlay remembered he didn't particularly like him, but he knew if anyone could help him make sense of all this, it was him.

He picked up the phone and started to dial. He sat with the phone to his ear, listening to the crackling on the line as it connected. He still wasn't sure if he was doing the right thing, but he had to admit, with Todd out of action, he needed help.

Suddenly, there was a voice he hadn't heard in years. "Hello?" it said.

"Hello," said Findlay, "is this Bob Newman? Sergeant Bob Newman?"

"It is," said the voice on the other end, "except it's just Bob Newman these days. I retired three years ago. Who's this?"

Findlay hesitated. "Bob," he said sharply, "hello, this is Findlay, Brian Findlay."

"Well I never," replied Newman. "It's been a long time."

"Yes, it has," replied Findlay.

"So what can I do for you?" said Newman.

Findlay told him all about the case he was working on and about the attack on his Sergeant. "I was wondering if you would mind taking a look?... but if you're retired…?"

Newman interrupted, "retired yes. Willing to help out? Definitely! I've spent the last three years wondering where my life had gone wrong. Don't believe everything you hear about putting your feet up old man! Are you still in Devon?"

"I am," said Findlay, "still in Torquay."

"Give me your address. I'll be on the first train in the morning from Paddington."

Findlay still wasn't sure if he was doing the right thing. He gave Newman the details, thanked him, and put the phone back on its hook.

Findlay lifted the file from his desk, tucked it under his arm, and made his way down to the street. He walked the short distance to Old Mill cottage where Sergeant Todd was now home after refusing to stay one more night in hospital.

He knocked gently on the door. Mrs Bruce opened it almost immediately. "Inspector!" she said, "come in."

"Thank you. Is it possible to have a word with Allan?"

Mrs Bruce didn't get a chance to answer, the sergeant shouted from the top of the stairs, "Inspector, come up!"

Findlay made his way up the brightly carpeted staircase and into his sergeant's room. "How are you?"

"I've been better, sir, but I'll live. I released myself, no point in taking up a hospital bed when I have one of my own."

Findlay told him about the visit from the two mystery men in the dark-coloured car and his call to Bob Newman.

"With you unable to work, I need some help," said Findlay. "Bob Newman was one of the best, he's retired now, but if anyone can help me sort this mess out, it's him."

He handed the file to Todd. "As you don't have a lot to do Sergeant, refresh your memory with this. I'll call back tomorrow morning. Maybe you will spot something I've missed."

———⊠———

Chapter 9

The next morning, Findlay decided to pay another visit to Jackson's sawmill. Something didn't add up. He just couldn't put his finger on it. He made his way back up the lane to Jackson's. Just as he arrived, the mill owner, Paul Jackson was driving out. The two men said nothing. They simply stared at each other as they passed.

Findlay sat for a moment looking up at Jackson's office. "Could be an opportunity," he mumbled to himself. Before he realised it, he was pushing open the glass doors to the reception. There was that smell again, he thought to himself, freshly cut timber.

"Can I help?" said a voice behind him. Findlay spun around,

"If you are looking for Mr Jackson, you've just missed him."

"I see," replied Findlay. "Maybe you could help? I've arranged a meeting with Mr Jackson. I am very early, I was wondering if maybe I could wait here? I have come an awfully long way."

Telling lies didn't sit well with him but if he was to make any headway, needs must, the chance of this man knowing him was remote.

"I don't know, I just work in the yard," said the man. "I don't suppose it would hurt. Save you another trip. Go on then, top of the stairs is his office. "

"That's very kind of you," replied Findlay, "thank you."

"I'm sure he will be back soon." The workman returned to his duties.

Findlay made his way up the creaky old wooden staircase to Jackson's office. Once inside, he began to feel very guilty. It wasn't in his nature to lie, but there was something that didn't feel right and he wanted to know what it was.

He glanced out of the window, nobody around, he thought. He made his way over to the filing cabinet from where Jackson had taken his ledger. He tugged on the top drawer. To his surprise, it was unlocked. He took out the ledger and placed it on Jackson's desk.

Findlay started to thumb through the pages. He didn't know what it was he was looking for. He just hoped it would jump out at him.

He reached the last page, nothing. He slowly began closing it when he remembered something. He opened the ledger at the back and there pencilled in on the very last page, DBJ37, that's what had been bugging him.

He had no idea what it meant, but his instinct was telling him it was important. He closed the ledger and walked over to the cabinet to replace it. There were at least a dozen or more files and ledgers. Findlay couldn't remember from which part of the drawer he had taken this one from.

"Wages," he muttered to himself, "W for wages." He started pushing back the files until he reached the space that said wages. He slotted the ledger into the space and was about to close it when suddenly, he saw it. A file headed Land Registry. Findlay pulled it out and opened it. "A survey map of Cockington village," he muttered, "why would he have detailed plans of the village?"

He unfolded one of the plans. It was Lanscombe Wood, the woods joined into Jackson's land. 'Why would he want these he thought to himself? Lanscombe is part of Cockington Village.' It was then he heard a car pull up, Findlay glanced out of the office side window, it was Jackson.

He quickly folded the area plans and put them back into the cabinet. 'Now here's the problem,' he thought,' there's one way in and one way out, plus the fact Jackson would have seen his car.' Findlay simply sat down. He picked up a magazine and began reading.

The door to Jackson's office swung open with a bang. "Inspector Findlay? May I ask what the hell you're doing here!?" said Jackson angrily.

"I've been waiting for you, sir," replied Findlay. "Your door was open, so I decided to just wait."

"Get out!" demanded Jackson.

"But I have some questions for you," said Findlay.

"Then make an appointment. Now get out!" demanded Jackson again.

"Very well sir, I'll leave, but I will be back."

At that, Findlay made his way to his car, thinking about how close he had come to getting caught. He made his way down to the village. He had just arrived at his office door when a taxi cab arrived, it was Bob Newman. Findlay couldn't help thinking he was looking old and hadn't aged well.

"Bob!" said Findlay. "Lovely to see you again, been a long time!"

"It has," replied Newman. "I'm surprised you're still out there catching the bad guys!"

Findlay smiled, "I do my best."

The two men made their way up to Findlay's office. Findlay pushed open the door and to his surprise, was greeted by Sergeant Todd.

"Sergeant," said Findlay, "what are you doing here!?"

"I was going mad sitting in my room, sir. I didn't think you would mind if I came in."

"Of course not. I'm pleased you feel well enough."

"Bob," said Findlay, "this is Sergeant Allan Todd."

"Sergeant Todd," said Newman. "I've heard a lot about you. I hope you are recovering from your accident?"

"Oh no sir," said Todd, "this was no accident. Whoever did this meant to do it. That car drove straight at me. It was intentional. "

Newman unbuttoned his coat. He removed his hat and scarf and hung them on the wooden coat stand in the corner. He looked Todd in the eye. "Why do you say that? What reason would anyone have to harm you? Did you get a look at them?"

Todd sighed, "Not really." He took a deep breath, "maybe I was asking too many questions? Somebody didn't like it."

"Questions?" asked Newman.

"Yes," replied Findlay, "the body that was found hanging at Cockington Court."

"Pardon me asking," said Todd, "have we met before? You look very familiar."

"I doubt it. I haven't been to Devon in over twenty years, so it's not likely."

"Sorry," said Todd, "you just look familiar."

"Not a problem Sergeant," said Newman.

Findlay opened the file and spread its contents around his desk.

"This, Bob, is all we have so far. "

Newman placed his hands on the desk and leaned over. After a few seconds, he looked up. "Not much to go on is it?"

Findlay slowly shook his head. "There is one other thing," he said quietly.

"Our Lord Mayor, Lipman, I have a feeling he's involved somewhere along the line. He's a despicable character. I expect you will get to meet him. I have some questions for him and Jackson, but this afternoon I need to have a word with Reverend Peters. "

"I could keep you company if you wish Inspector?" said Newman with a grin.

"That's okay, Sergeant Todd and I can manage this. You get yourself down to The Drum. I have already rung them, they are expecting you."

"Well gentlemen, in that case, that will do for now. I presume your village pub does food?"

"It does," said Todd enthusiastically. "I'll take you down there if you like?"

"I don't think so," said Findlay." Now you're back at work, it would be rather nice if you actually did some work, and that doesn't mean a visit to the pub."

"Of course Inspector," replied Todd, "of course."

"Quite alright," said Newman, "I'm sure Sally will look after me!"

Newman picked up the assortment of notes from the desk and placed them back into the file. "I'll go through these tonight," said Newman, "bring myself up to scratch, and I will see you around ten in the morning."

The two men shook hands and Newman left. Findlay stood for a while and watched him walking down the hill to the Drum Inn.

"You're very quiet sir," said Todd.

"Am I Sergeant? I was just thinking, did you mention anything to Bob about Sally?"

"No sir, I don't think so. No reason why I should."

"Strange," said Findlay. "So you had a feeling you had met him before?"

"Yes I did sir, I was obviously mistaken."

"Hmm," said Findlay, "obviously."

"Right Sergeant, let's take a drive. There's something I want to have a look at."

The two men made their way down to Findlay's car. They headed out of the village and towards Torquay town. They had only gone for a mile or so and Findlay stopped at the front of Chelston Church.

"Out you get," said Findlay.

"Sir," exclaimed Todd, "why the church?"

"It's just a hunch, something I saw in Jackson's mill."

The two men made their way to the old church. Sergeant Todd pushed open the heavy door. As it opened it swung back and hit the old granite walls with a thud.

The sound echoed around the church. "Steady on Sergeant," said Findlay, "that's an eight hundred-year-old door."

"Sorry," said Todd.

They made their way to the vestry at the back of the church. "Reverend?" shouted Findlay.

"Reverend?" he shouted again.

Still no reply.

"Doesn't seem to be anyone here, sir."

"No, Sergeant, but there should be. I know Reverend Peters, he wouldn't leave the church unattended and unlocked."

"I'll check outside sir, he may be out back." Todd made his way to the back door and went out into the church gardens.

Findlay left the vestry and walked towards the small kitchen area around the side of the building. He pushed open the door. There to his horror, was Reverend Peters. He had been tied to a wooden chair, hands behind his back. He had been beaten.

"Oh my god!" shouted Findlay. He could see instantly that Peters had been severely beaten. The reverend was small in stature and very slight of build.

Findlay started removing the ropes from the Reverend Peters' hands, "who did this to you?"

Reverend Peters' head was down. He said nothing as the blood ran down his face from a deep gash on his head. Findlay went down on his knees and started to remove the ropes from his feet. It was then he noticed a cleat knot; the same knot that had bound the feet of Gregson, the body in Cockington Court.

Just then, Todd came through the door." Oh my god, is he okay?"

"I don't know, there's a phone in the vestry, ring an ambulance."

"Yes, sir!"

"Quickly, Sergeant. Quickly!"

Findlay took a towel from the hook on the door and began wiping the blood from the reverend's face. "Who did this to you?"

Peters raised his head slowly and said, "I don't know Inspector. I was hit from behind."

"Were you robbed?"

"I don't think so. They just kept asking me where the church ledgers were kept. They kept asking me over and over."

'Why would they want those?' Findlay thought to himself. Just then, the door opened.

Sergeant Todd entered, "Ambulance is on its way, sir."

"Did they get the ledgers?" asked Findlay.

"Yes, they did. I wasn't about to be hit again to save a few old books. I don't understand. Why would they do this? And why on earth would anybody want to steal old church records?"

"I don't know," said Findlay, "but I will find out."

"You're sure you didn't recognise them?" asked Todd.

"I'm sure Sergeant," replied Reverend Peters, "it all happened so quickly."

"Did you hear any names?" asked Findlay, "anything that could help?"

"No, I'm afraid not Inspector, I'm sorry. "

It was then they heard the wail of the ambulance siren. "You'll be alright reverend," said Findlay, putting a hand on his shoulder." The ambulance is here, they will take care of you."

"Thank you Inspector," said the reverend.

Findlay and Todd were about to leave when the reverend suddenly said, "Scottish."

Findlay spun around. "What did you say Reverend?"

"Scottish, one of them had a Scottish accent."

Findlay just stared at him. "Are you sure?"

"Yes," said Peters, "…quite sure. Yes. I'm sure."

Findlay and Todd made their way back to the car.

"None of this is making any sense Sergeant, why steal old church records, and what kind of people would do that to an old man? A churchman at that."

"It takes all sorts, sir," said Todd.

The two men climbed into the car. Findlay sat, hands on the steering wheel, staring out of the window. Todd said nothing. He had known him long enough to know when to keep quiet.

After a while, Todd broke the silence. He took a deep breath and said, "I've been thinking, sir."

"Really, Sergeant?" said Findlay.

"Yes sir. I was just thinking, a mystery is only a mystery while it remains investigated."

Findlay raised his eyebrows and slowly turned to face his sergeant. "That is probably the most profound thing you've ever said Sergeant."

"Is it, sir?"

"No, not really."

Findlay put his car into gear and they made their way to the village.

Both men were quiet, until suddenly Findlay said, "Town Hall."

"Town Hall?" repeated Todd.

"Yes, a copy of the church records going back hundreds of years, are kept in the Town Hall vault. That's why they went for the church. No way could they get into the vault. The church only keeps copies. Originals are kept in the town hall vault."

"We need to see those records, maybe get some answers."

"Answers to what, sir?"

"Answers as to why somebody would assault a man of the cloth and steal church records." Findlay turned into the lane and headed towards Torquay town centre.

———≫⋈≪———

Chapter 10

I t wasn't long before they reached the town. Findlay parked the car and the two men crossed the road and walked towards the town hall, an imposing building built in the mid-eighteenth century.

The two men climbed the steps and entered, their footsteps echoed around the whole building. Todd stopped in his tracks. "What's wrong?" said Findlay.

"I haven't been in here for years," whispered Todd. "We used to come here when we were kids. We would run in the front door and hoot like owls, the echoes lasted forever. The old watchman used to chase us," said Todd. "Never caught us."

"So," said Findlay, "not always been law abiding then?"

"No sir, not always."

They made their way up the marble steps leading to the council offices. "Over there sir," said Todd, "reception."

Findlay pushed open the door. "Yes?" said a very stern-looking lady behind the desk. "What can I do for you?"

"I'm…"

"I know who you are Inspector. Mayor Lipman said you would probably be calling. Go straight in. "

The two men looked at each other. "Well, I suppose we better go in."

They pushed open the glass-fronted door with Mayor's Office stamped in gold letters on it. There sitting behind a large leather-topped desk, was Lipman.

"Well, well, inspector, we meet again, and so soon."

Findlay said nothing. He turned to his sergeant and quietly said, "Close the door, would you?"

"Yes sir," said Todd.

"Please," said Lipman, "take a seat. What can I do for you?"

"There's been an attack," said Findlay.

"Yes, I heard. Terrible state of affairs when a man of the cloth is assaulted?"

"How did you know that?" said Todd.

"News travels fast sergeant, it's my job to know what's going on."

"It seems they were after the church records."

"Oh?" said Lipman. "Why would anybody want old church records?"

"I don't know yet," said Findlay, "but I will find out."

"Originals are kept in the Town Hall vaults, I believe?"

"Yes," said Lipman.

"Then I would like to take a look at them."

"For what reason Inspector?"

"Because I would," said Findlay with a glare.

"I'm afraid I can't allow that," said Lipman, "not without a court order or permission from the council. You do have a court order, don't you Inspector?"

Findlay didn't reply, he just stood up. "I will be back."

"Sergeant."

"Yes sir," said Todd, opening the door. He was about to close it behind them when he noticed the smile on Mayor Lipman's face.

He decided not to mention it to Inspector Findlay. He could see the anger already building in him. They made their way down the winding marble staircase, their footsteps echoing around the huge entrance hall. Findlay said nothing as he took the town hall steps two at a time towards his car.

"What now?" said Todd.

"Now we get a search warrant, and you sergeant, you go to the Pub."

Todd's eyes opened wide. "The pub sir?"

"Yes, the pub. Go to The Drum in the village. See how Bob Newman is getting on. See if he can think of a reason anyone would want old church records?"

"I will see you back at the office around two this afternoon. Bring Newman with you."

Findlay climbed into the driver's seat, leaned over and pushed open the passenger door. "Well, get in, unless you're planning on walking back."

Todd climbed in. Findlay just shook his head.

Chapter 11

They made their way back to Cockington Village. Not a word was said. Findlay pulled up at the Drum Inn. "Two o'clock."

"Of course, sir," said Todd as he climbed out.

Findlay drove off up the hill to his office. Todd couldn't believe his luck. He pushed open the heavy oak door to the pub, and there, standing behind the bar in front of him was Sally.

"Well, well, well," she said sarcastically, "early start, isn't it?"

"I'm here on police business Sally."

"Oh really? You'll not be wanting a pint then?" she said. "Haven't you forgiven me yet Alan?"

Todd bit his bottom lip. "I don't know yet, Sal," he replied.

He stood for a second. Then he said, "go on then, just the one."

Sally lifted a glass and filled it to the brim. "On the house," she whispered.

"Very kind of you," said Todd. He took a long drink from the pot and stood for a few seconds. "I needed that!" he said with a grin.

"So you're here on police business?"

"Yes, I am Sally. Would you be kind enough to call Mr Newman? I need him to accompany me to Inspector Findlay's office."

Sally was about to shout up the stairs when she heard, "I'm here Sergeant."

Todd swung around with a start. There, sitting in one of the cubicles, was Bob Newman.

"Sorry sir," said Todd, "I didn't see you."

Todd told him the inspector wanted to see them at two o'clock.

"Not a problem. Help me collect all this paperwork together and I will be more than happy to go with you."

Todd began collecting together the paperwork scattered around the table.

"Don't forget your beer Sergeant," said Newman, "there's no rush."

"Do you have such a thing as a working police car?"

"We do," said Todd. "But it's not been out of the garage for at least a year. The inspector likes to use his own car."

Newman smiled and slowly shook his head, "of course he does Sergeant."

"Ready?" said Newman.

"Yes sir, of course," replied Todd.

Newman made his way to the door. Sergeant?"

"I'm coming," replied Todd, placing his empty pint pot on the bar.

The two men made their way up the hill to a small lock-up garage next door to Findlay's office. Todd reached up and took down the garage key from above the door. Newman shook his head and smiled.

"Who's going to steal a police car?" said Todd with a grin.

Newman again shook his head and pulled open the wooden doors. There to his surprise, was a modern-looking police car. A black mark three Jaguar complete with a shiny new bell. "I'm impressed. Does it run?"

"I've no idea sir, I've never used it. We don't get much call around here for car chases."

"Can I ask sir, where are we going? I'm supposed to be taking you to see the inspector."

Newman took the file Todd was holding. He pulled out the papers and spread them on the bonnet of the car. "Right Sergeant," said Newman, opening a map of the village.

He pointed to Scanlon Woods. "This area here, it's the only part of the village not owned by the sawmills according to the plans."

"I know sir," said Todd, "the woods were left to the village by lord Cockington decades ago, long before the sawmills."

"Take me there."

"But sir," stuttered Todd, "what about Inspector Findlay?"

"I'm sure your inspector will understand."

Todd raised his eyebrows, "yes sir, if you say so."

Newman opened the car door and climbed into the driver's seat. "Right Sergeant, fingers crossed."

He turned the key, and the engine burst into life. Newman nodded his head. "That's twice in as many minutes I've been impressed Sergeant."

The two men set off for Scanlon Woods. Before long, they reached the clearing that led into a heavily wooded area. "Seems we have to walk the rest of the way, sir."

Todd climbed out. "What exactly is it we are looking for?"

"Nothing in particular, I just wanted to have a look."

The two men walked slowly and quietly into the woods. All that could be heard was birdsong and the tap of a distant woodpecker.

"You're new here, aren't you Sergeant?"

"Not really sir, I've been here over seven years."

"That's what I meant," said Newman, "seven years makes you the new boy. How do you get on with the inspector? Do you mix with him outside work? Are you friends or is it just a job?"

"We don't really mix. The Inspector doesn't drink. He isn't one for socialising," said Todd. "But yes, I would say we were friends. After all, there's only the two of us here."

Newman nodded.

"Why do you ask sir?" said Todd.

"No reason, I was just interested," said Newman.

"I believe you knew him before he came to Cockington?" said Todd.

Newman didn't reply.

"Sir?" said Todd.

"Yes Sergeant, I heard you."

"Tell me Sergeant, do you trust him?"

"Absolutely," replied Todd without a second thought. "Why do you ask?"

Again Newman said nothing. He just turned and made his way back to the car.

"Come along Sergeant!" shouted Newman, "I've seen what I wanted to see, next stop, the village."

"Yes sir," said Todd, "the inspector will be waiting."

"No Sergeant, take me back to the pub."

"But sir," said Todd.

"The pub!" snapped Newman.

The two men made their way back along the winding country lane towards the village, nothing was said. Todd was beginning to see what kind of man Newman was, so he said nothing. Something told him he couldn't trust him.

Chapter 12

Meanwhile, inspector Findlay was sitting patiently in the Judge's chambers waiting for his search warrant. He sat very still and stared at the clock above the office door. He couldn't help but notice how loud the tick tock tick tock was, and the occasional hiss from the radiator at the side of him. He could feel his eyes slowly closing and his head sinking lower and lower.

Suddenly, a door opened. Findlay was startled and quickly raised himself from his seat. "Inspector." said a very stern-looking receptionist, "your warrant."

"Thank you," stammered Findlay, "thank you." He briefly glanced at his warrant, folded it, and put it into his jacket pocket.

He made his way to the exit. He couldn't help but smile. 'It isn't often,' he thought, 'that I get one over on Lipman, but today's the day.'

He made his way back to the town hall, still smiling. He even found himself humming a tune as he made his way up the marble staircase leading to Mayor Lipman's office.

He reached the glass doorway, stood for a few seconds, straightened his tie and pushed open the door. He stood in the doorway, arm outstretched, holding the newly issued court order.

"Lipman!" he shouted, as he stepped into the office, "here's your court order."

Findlay stood for a few seconds and looked around. No Lipman. "Damn!" he muttered under his breath.

He turned around and slammed the door behind him. Findlay made his way back down the marble staircase and out into the bright sunshine. He stood for a moment at the top of the steps leading to the town hall.

"Damn," he said out loud. It was then he heard a car horn. It was Sergeant Todd.

Findlay made his way down to the car. "Sergeant," he said in an abrupt voice.

"Sir," said Todd, "I have to speak with you."

"Not now Sergeant, I have to find Lipman."

"No sir," said Todd, "now, it's important."

Findlay took a deep breath and slowly let it out. "Very well Sergeant, what's so important?"

Todd sat quietly for a few seconds.

"Well?" shouted Findlay, "speak up man."

"You remember when I had my accident, when I was hit by the car?"

"Yes," said Findlay.

"Well, I didn't get a good look at the driver, it was dark and raining."

"Yes yes, get to the point."

"Well sir," said Todd, "I did get a quick look at the passenger."

"Yes, and?"

"And sir, I know who it was."

Findlay turned and stared at his sergeant. "Go on," he said slowly.

"Well sir, it was Bob Newman, I'm sure of it. It was only for a second, but it was him."

Findlay glared at him. Then started to laugh.

"I'm serious sir, it was him. Remember when you introduced us? I said, then his face was familiar."

"That's ridiculous," snapped Findlay. "If I hadn't rung him, he wouldn't even be here, I hadn't seen him for years."

"I know what I saw," said Todd, "it was him, I would stake my life on it."

"There's something else, sir."

"What now Sergeant?"

"Well sir, I contacted an old friend of mine in Exeter nick. I got him to do some checking for me, he's just come back. The car that hit me and the car you saw that night are the same. I gave him the registration letters DB7. They came back as DBJ 37. It's the only DB plate registered. They match, it's the same car."

Findlay sat quietly and stared out of the window. "How is that possible? He knew nothing about the case until I rang him."

"Only one way to find out sir, ask him. If he is somehow involved in this, I want to know, I still can't lift my arm over my head!"

"Hmm," said Findlay, "very strange. "

"Right, first things first. I have a court order to serve, let's find Tom Lipman. Then we will have a word with Bob Newman, he will be at the Drum. "

The two made their way back to the village in silence. They headed straight for The Drum Inn. They pulled up outside. Still not a word was said, Todd pushed open the old heavy oak front door.

The bar was empty, not unusual at lunchtime. It was then that Findlay spotted the cigarette smoke rising from one of the cubicles. He walked slowly over. Sat in the corner of the old wooden cubical was Bob Newman and to Findlay's amazement, Mayor Lipman.

"Mr Mayor," said Findlay angrily. "I've just come from your office."

"I'm not there," Lipman replied with a smirk.

Findlay said nothing, he just glared at Lipman.

A few seconds passed which to sergeant Todd felt like a lifetime. He was about to break the silence when Findlay turned to Bob Newman. "I wasn't aware you and our town Mayor were acquainted?"

Newman sat and stared at his beer for a second. "And I wasn't aware I had to have permission," he replied.

"I was going through the paperwork you gave me. I had a few questions that needed answering, so I rang Mayor Lipman and he arranged to meet me here."

Findlay glanced back at Lipman, who was still smiling.

"Seems my sergeant has seen you before Bob."

"Really?" replied Newman. "Well, I still have friends here. Maybe you have seen me in here?"

"Yes sir," replied Todd, "possibly. I seem to remember you saying you hadn't been to Devon in some years, Bob?"

"It's been a while, yes," replied Newman.

"Then it wasn't in here!" snapped Findlay.

Sergeant Todd was about to speak up when Findlay stopped him. He pulled the court order from his pocket and dropped it on the table in front of Mayor Lipman.

"What's this?" said Lipman.

"It's the order I promised you, giving me access to the town hall vaults."

Lipman lost his smile and Findlay could see he was shaken. He picked it up and opened it. "I thought you were only interested in the church records?"

"I was," replied Findlay. "That order gives me the power to look at anything and everything."

Lipman folded the papers up. "Very well Inspector, tomorrow morning."

"No," said Findlay, "NOW! "

"Anything you say Inspector."

He stood up, finished his drink, then made his way to the front door with Sergeant Todd and Findlay following.

Outside, Lipman walked to his car. "This way Mr Mayor!" shouted Findlay, "in our car. Todd will drop you back, wouldn't want you getting there before us, would we?"

They climbed in and made their way back to the town hall. Not much was said until " how's the vicar doing?" said Lipman.

Sergeant Todd glanced over at Findlay, he could see he was in no mood for conversation. "I said, how's the vicar doing after his accident?"

"It wasn't an accident," said Todd.

Lipman tutted and shook his head.

The three men soon arrived back at the Town Hall. First out of the car was Mayor Lipman. Findlay jumped out and caught up with him as they made their way up the steps to the entrance hall.

"I'm going to enjoy this," said Findlay. "I don't know what it is you're trying to hide, but I will find it."

"Now, vault keys," demanded Findlay, holding out his hand.

Lipman handed over the vault keys. Findlay snatched them. "Sergeant Todd is parking the car," he said, "when he arrives send him down."

At that, Findlay walked into the entrance hall and made his way down the cold marble stairway leading to the Town Hall vaults.

He was about to open the vault door when Todd arrived. "Right Sergeant, let us get this done."

They pushed open the vault door and entered. Findlay took out his handkerchief and held it to his nose. "What's that smell?"

"History sir," replied Todd, "hundreds of years of history, and the smell of rats, I think. Should I open a window sir? Let some air in?"

Findlay shook his head, "sometimes I am lost for words. This is one of those times."

"Sir," mumbled Todd.

"It's a vault Sergeant, some twenty feet underground. Where would you find a window?"

Todd thought for a second then raised one eyebrow and smiled, "of course sir, I didn't think."

Findlay shook his head, "Sit, the answer to this puzzle is in here. All we have to do is find it."

———⋈———

Chapter 13

F indlay took a small black book from his inside pocket and removed a small red pencil.

"Right, Sergeant, let's look at the facts. We have one suicide, which we now know was murder. So why would anybody kill a small-time crook? And why make it look like a suicide?"

"Then there was the attack on the church. Whatever they were after was important enough to assault the vicar."

"Then there's George Mallock, and let's not forget Lipman, horrible little man. Where does he fit into all this? And then there's Jackson from the sawmill. Somehow, he's involved, I just know it."

"Not forgetting Bob Newman Sir," said Todd," I know it was him in that car, I just know it.

Findlay shook his head, "maybe Sergeant, maybe."

Todd stood up, "there's no maybe sir, I know it was him."

Findlay yanked open a filing cabinet and pulled out a handful of documents.

"Here Sergeant, look through these, you are looking for anything to do with Lanscome Woods."

"Meanwhile, I will go through the church records."

The two men spent the entire afternoon thumbing through old records and parchments, but nothing really made any sense.

"What's the time Sergeant?"

"It's after seven sir."

"Is it really? Mrs Findlay will think I've left home. Leave everything as it is," said Findlay." We will be back tomorrow."

Findlay stood and started to put his coat on, then stopped.

"What's wrong Sir?"

"33D Sergeant."

"What does it mean, sir?"

"I don't know, but I saw it on a set of plans in Jackson's office. I think I've just seen it again, it just didn't register."

He threw off his coat and pulled a box full of rolled-up paper across the table.

"Here, look through these. Somewhere is an entry, 33D."

Todd started to unroll the old scrolls of paper. One by one, they went through each of them. Suddenly Todd broke the silence, 233D3, is that it, sir!"

"That's it, perfect!" Findlay unrolled the scroll. "It's the area plans for Cockington and the village, but what does 33D3 mean?"

Todd hovered over the scroll with his head tilted to one side. "It looks almost like a road reference?"

"A what?" asked Findlay.

"A map reference sir, like the B303."

"Of course!" said Findlay. "Pass me the church record book."

Findlay opened the book on the reference page and ran his finger down the long list. Suddenly, he stopped. "It's not a road, it's the old church reference for the area now taken up by Jackson's sawmill. Where's the planning permission applications?"

"Here they are, sir."

Findlay again ran his finger down the list of applications," got it, 33D3. It's an application for the purchase of Lanscome Woods, by Jackson's sawmill. And look at this, they're planning to build a motorway from Plymouth to Exeter, and it runs right through Lanscome Wood. That land will be worth a king's ransom to whoever owns it. Worth killing for Sergeant!"

"Now let's see who made the application."

Findlay went quiet.

"You ok, sir?"

"Yes," said Findlay, "I think so. It seems you may have been right! The name on the planning application is Robert Newman. Bob. How can he be involved? I rang him out of the blue, I don't understand."

"Only one way to find out, sir."

"You're right. Collect all this together and meet me back at my office in half an hour. I'm going to see Newman at the Drum Inn."

Todd began folding and rolling what was now evidence and placed it all into a cardboard box.

Findlay made his way back up the dark marble staircase. He was almost at the top when there, standing in front of him, stood a figure. He squinted, trying to make out who it was, but all he could see was a silhouette against the brightness of the hall lights.

"Hello?" said Findlay, "what can I do for you?"

The stranger said nothing.

Findlay slowly climbed the stairs, getting closer to the figure in the doorway. Suddenly, he heard Todd running up behind him. Findlay leaned to one side and pressed himself against the dry dusty plaster of the vault walls.

Todd lunged at the figure, which was now trying to close the vault door. Todd barely made it before the door slammed shut. He threw his arm into the small opening. "Argh!" shrieked Todd, "my arm. Not again!" he shouted.

He pushed with all his might, but whoever this was on the other side was a lot heavier and stronger. Todd knew if the door closed, they would be in serious trouble and have no way to get out. It was then he spotted the handgun.

He pushed and pushed. Suddenly the door flew open and with it went Todd. To his amazement, standing in front of him holding a fire extinguisher was Lipman, the town Mayor.

———≺✕≻———

Chapter 14

F indlay slowly came through the door. "Are you alright?"

"Yes sir, I think so," said Todd, nursing his left arm.

Findlay stood for a second or two, looking at Lipman. "Did you do this?"

"Yes," said Lipman. He glanced at the Inspector. "I suppose I did, yes. "

"Two words I never thought I would say to you, Mr Mayor," said Findlay, "thank you!"

Lipman said nothing. He just stood and nodded his head.

"Who is it?" said Lipman.

"I have no idea. Sergeant, do you recognise him?"

"No sir, never seen him before."

"Have I killed him?" said Lipman quietly.

"No, he's breathing. Call an ambulance," said Findlay, "and Sergeant, handcuff him and bag that revolver. Oh, and Sergeant, carefully, don't touch it!"

"No sir," replied Todd.

"I need to speak with Mayor Lipman, keep an eye on the prisoner, Sergeant."

"Yes, sir."

The two men made their way up to Mayor Lipman's office and went inside.

They stood and faced each other in silence. "Well," said Findlay, "what's going on?"

"I don't have any real proof yet, but I know you're involved somehow with this land deal."

"I might be a lot of things, Inspector, but I'm no killer," replied Lipman. "I just knew you would piece it together once you got hold of the land and property applications."

"So how is Bob Newman involved?"

Lipman stood quietly, not knowing what to do for the best outcome. Then he said, "Coincidence. He's been involved since the beginning. When you phoned him, well, it was a gift. Pure coincidence that you should contact him."

"Did he kill Gregson?"

"Who?" said Lipman.

"Steven Gregson, the supposed suicide at the manor."

"Oh," said Lipman, "no, he didn't."

"Well, if he didn't, who did?"

"Jackson," he said quietly, "Jackson arranged it."

"Gregson found out about the proposed motorway and that Jackson was paying off some high ups in local government to help him buy Mallock farm. Plus, the land around it running right through Cockington Village and Lanscome Woods. He has been blackmailing Jackson for months. Jackson was giving him odd jobs at the mill and paying him crazy money."

"Gregson got greedy. He wanted more. So Jackson hired the two heavies, nasty pieces of work to sort the problem out. I thought they would just work him over and warn him off. Jackson found them on Torquay harbour. Sailors from a cargo ship, one German and the other a Scot. You have to believe me, I knew nothing about what they intended to do."

Findlay turned to Todd, "that explains the knot, of course, sailors. "

He glared at Lipman. "Go on," he said sternly.

"Jackson offered me five thousand pounds to push the paperwork through the council. I didn't know he was capable of murder or arranging it. I might not be honest Inspector, but I'll have nothing to do with murder, or trying to kill a police officer."

Todd spun around. "You mean Jackson had me run over, almost killed?"

"I'm afraid he did Sergeant. The night you were hit by the car, it was one of his henchmen and Newman."

"I knew it!" shouted Todd. "I knew I had seen him before!" Todd turned around and started for the exit.

"Sergeant!" shouted Findlay, "what are you doing?"

"I'm going to the mill. I owe Jackson!"

"Stop right there!" demanded Findlay, "all in good time."

He turned to face Lipman. "Sergeant, take the mayor into custody. Lock him in his office for now."

"It's for your own safety," said Findlay with a smirk, "and sergeant, remove the telephone. We wouldn't want Mr Jackson getting wind of our conversation, would we?"

"I think Mr Mayor that your days of politics are over."

"But I've told you everything, doesn't that count for anything?"

Findlay looked him in the eye and simply said, "No".

"Remember the day you threatened my family? I said you would pay for that one day, and that day is now. Sergeant, lock him up and meet me at the car. We need to pay Mr Jackson a visit."

———◇———

Chapter 15

The two men made their way up the winding tree-lined lane of Lanscome Woods towards the sawmills. They were halfway there when coming towards them was a large black car.

"Sir!" exclaimed Todd, "the registration, DB and 7, it's them. It's the car that hit me!"

Todd hit the brakes hard and skidded to stop. The black car instead of slowing down, seemed to speed up. "Out Sergeant! Get out," shouted Findlay.

The two men threw open the car doors and jumped for their lives. Todd landed hard on the gravel lane and rolled as far as he could. Findlay hit the grass verge with a thud and scampered up the embankment. The black car veered off to try to squeeze down the side. There simply wasn't enough space and it smashed into the front of Findlay's pride and joy.

Findlay shuffled on his backside down the grass embankment, still dazed.

"Sergeant!" he shouted, "Sergeant Todd, are you alright?"

"Yes," came the reply, "I'm over here!"

They both walked out onto the lane to see their car had been destroyed. The black car was sandwiched between the grass verge and the Volvo tilted up on two wheels.

Suddenly, the driver's side door was kicked open. Todd and Findlay stared at the open door, waiting to see who was going to come out.

"Should I help?" said Todd.

"I suppose we should," said Findlay. "Go on then. Up you get, let's see who just tried to kill us."

He climbed up onto the side of the car and peered into its interior. There, staring back at him, was Bob Newman. Newman reached out his hand, Todd grasped it and pulled.

Findlay looked on in amazement as Bob Newman slowly appeared. The two men carefully lowered themselves to the ground. "This isn't what it seems," said Newman."

"I think it's exactly as it seems," replied Findlay.

"What!" exclaimed Newman. "You think I deliberately tried to hit you?"

"Yes," said Findlay, "I do."

"I was stamping on the brakes, but it wouldn't stop! Thank God I didn't get to the bottom of the hill in the village. It simply wouldn't stop. Jackson's manager gave me a lift up there from the Drum. He told me I could use it to get back and when I was finished, and he would collect it."

"The brakes have been tampered with sir," said Todd. "There's brake fluid all over the road."

Findlay crouched down to have a look.

"Well?" said Bob Newman, "an apology would be nice."

Findlay looked at Todd, then at Newman, and then at his Volvo. "A case of no honour among thieves, more like. Look at my car! I spent two hours polishing that yesterday. Now look at it!"

Todd jumped in with, "it could have been worse."

Findlay glared at him, "how so?" he said with a gasp.

"We could have been in it sir, so it could have been worse."

Findlay shook his head, "Sergeant," he said, "shut up."

He turned to Bob Newman. "We've just had a long chat with the mayor. He told us everything, so your lies are wasted on me. I'm looking for a killer, and the way things stand, your name is top of the list."

"That's ridiculous!" said Newman. "I wouldn't even be here if it wasn't for your phone call."

"That's what I thought," said Findlay, "but then the mayor told me all about you and Jackson's plans to buy Scanlon Woods, and sell it on for a huge profit to our highways department. "

"WHAT! That's ludicrous. You don't actually believe him? Oh my god?! You do! You think I'm involved! Where's Mayor Lipman now?"

Todd stepped forward, "I locked him in his office."

"His office?" said Newman, shaking his head, "unbelievable."

He turned to Findlay. "Take me to him. I'll prove I had nothing to do with this."

"Sergeant!" shouted Findlay, "over here!"

The three men now stood in front of the car Newman was driving.

"Ready?" said Findlay, "push!"

The three of them pushed with all their might. Slowly it began to roll backwards until eventually, with a bang, it dropped onto all four wheels. Findlay could now see his beloved Volvo. It did not do much to improve his mood.

He climbed into the driver's seat and turned the key. Even in the sad state it was in, the engine started first time. Findlay bit his bottom lip and shook his head. "I knew you wouldn't let me down, old girl," he muttered.

"Well, come along!" he shouted, "get in!"

Todd opened the front passenger door and climbed in. Newman just stood in the lane, Findlay looked over his shoulder, "Are you coming or not?" he shouted at Newman. At that Newman climbed into the back and they set off for Mayor Lipman's office.

Nothing was said on the way back to Torquay. When they arrived, Todd was first out of the car, followed by Newman and then Inspector Findlay.

Todd looked up towards Mayor Lipman's office. "The lights are out," said Todd.

"I can't imagine him sitting in the dark," said Newman.

They made their way up the marble and granite staircase towards the mayor's office. Findlay couldn't help thinking how creepy it was at night. He had only ever been there during the daytime. The noise of the three men hurrying up the stairs echoed around the empty building, every footstep bouncing back at them.

They reached Lipman's office, which was indeed in darkness. Todd slowly turned the door handle, which made a ratcheting sound that echoed down the hallway. He slowly pushed open the office door and reached in to turn on the lights. Click, went the light switch, but still darkness. Click, click, it went again as Todd flicked it on and off.

Findlay pushed his way in." Lipman!" he shouted angrily. But there was nobody to be seen. "Damn that man!" barked Findlay.

"I don't understand sir, I locked him in, I know I did."

"Keys," said Findlay.

Todd held the keys out for Findlay to take. "No, spare keys. Lipman obviously had spare keys."

"Oh yes sir, of course," said Todd, slowly lowering his arm and feeling like yet again he had made himself look foolish.

Newman broke the silence, "Inspector, over here."

Findlay walked slowly over to the window, "there's your Mayor Inspector," said Newman, pointing to the street below.

The three men quickly made their way to the street. It was Mayor Lipman lying in a pool of blood. Findlay went down on one knee and checked for a pulse. Nothing, it was too late.

"At least I can't be blamed for this one," said Newman sarcastically.

Findlay shook his head.

"What do you think, sir? Pushed or jumped?" Questioned Todd.

"No idea. Either way, it's a long way down. I thought the man was despicable, but I wouldn't have wished this on him."

Newman said nothing. He just stared at the lifeless body of Mayor Lipman.

"You never get used to it, do you?" said Findlay.

Suddenly, the three men spun around as they heard the roar of a car's engine. Todd ran down the steps of the town hall, trying to get to it before it had the chance to escape, but it was too fast for him.

Findlay and Newman quickly joined him. "Did you get a look at them?" said Newman.

"No sir, they were too quick, but I did get this," he said holding out his notepad, DBJ 37.

"It's the same car that ran me down!"

"And," said Findlay, "the same car that was parked outside my house."

"Quickly," said Findlay, "bring the car around, they can't get far!"

Todd ran to get the car. Findlay turned to Newman. "I'm sorry Bob. Lipman was very convincing. I shouldn't have doubted you."

Newman said nothing for a few seconds. He just stared at the lifeless body lying in the street.

He took a deep breath and said, "Jackson, it has to be Jackson!"

Findlay nodded, "it looks that way."

Todd pulled the car up. "I've rung for an ambulance and contacted the station at Paignton. They will be here shortly."

"Well done Sergeant," said Findlay.

At that, the Ambulance arrived. The three men climbed into the car. "Jackson's Mill," said Findlay, "and step on it Sergeant!"

They set off in search of the black car and headed for Cockington. They soon reached Lanscombe Lane, which wound its way around the back of the sawmill.

Before long, they stopped at the top of Lanscombe Woods, which look down onto the mill.

"There's the car," said Findlay.

The three men began picking their way down the steep incline, hanging onto tree roots and rocks as their feet slipped on the wet grass.

After what seemed an age, they were on the ground behind Jackson's office.

Findlay looked up, an open window he said, "right Sergeant, you're the youngest. Up you go and unlock this rear door, and don't get caught."

"You want me to climb up there and crawl in through a window Mrs Bruce's cat would struggle to get through?"

"Yes," said Findlay, "come along Sergeant, up you go."

Todd pulled himself up onto a thin ledge just below the open window. He reached up and partly pulled and wriggled his way up the wall. He grabbed the window ledge and pulled himself in through the narrow opening.

A short time passed and the rear door opened. "Well done Sergeant," said Bob Newman, "I knew you could do it."

Todd shook his head and beckoned them in. They made their way along a sparsely lit, windowless corridor, every step sent up a plume of sawdust. They reached the door at the end, "now listen you two," whispered Findlay, "on the other side of this door are the steps leading up to Jackson's office."

"Sergeant you go up first…"

"I know," said Todd, "I'm the youngest."

"Correct," said Findlay.

"Before you go Sergeant, you were right. I was in the car, but you have to believe me, I had no idea he was going to run you down. I said nothing when I found out you were going to be okay. Jackson threatened me if I opened my mouth. This land deal is worth millions to him. He would stop at nothing, even setting his henchmen onto me."

Todd said nothing. He just shrugged his shoulders.

Findlay quietly and slowly opened the door. There in front of them stood Jackson and two strangers. "Inspector, I've been expecting you! You've become quite an irritant!"

One of the strangers took his hand from his pocket. He was holding a revolver and pointed it at Todd. In a heavy accent he said, "whatever you're thinking, don't."

"Do as he says Sergeant."

"Now move! Upstairs," said Jackson, "all of you, move!"

They made their way up to Jackson's office. The three men stood to one side while the gun was still pointing at Sergeant Todd.

"You just couldn't leave it alone, could you?" said Jackson. "Months of planning and you ruin it."

"What are you going to do with us?" asked Findlay.

"This deal is worth millions over the next two years," said Jackson. He looked over at the two strangers. "I don't want to do this, but you've left me no choice."

Jackson looked at Newman. "What do you say Bob? Do we get rid of them?"

At that, Bob Newman crossed the room and joined Jackson and his two henchmen.

Newman smiled, "you're so gullible," he said, looking straight at Findlay.

"You rat!" shouted Sergeant Tod. "It was you who killed Mayor Lipman!"

"No," said Newman. "I'm only in it for the money. I'm no killer. I couldn't believe it when you rang me out of the blue! As it happens, you've been very helpful; you give me information, and I tell Mr Jackson and his rather dangerous friends here."

"Lipman was getting in the way," said Jackson. "It was very accommodating of you, Sergeant Todd, locking him in his office instead of the local holding cell. I told them to frighten him, seems he tried to escape, they struggled, and he fell out of the window."

"And Gregson?" said Findlay.

"Oh yes, the suicide at Cockington Court. He got greedy. Every week, he demanded more money to keep quiet, so he had to be dealt with. But now, what are we going to do with you two?" Asked Jackson.

No sooner had the words left his lips than Todd lunged at the man holding the revolver. Findlay dived at Bob Newman. He was no fighter.

The four men rolled around on the floor of Jackson's office, sawdust filled the air like choking smog. Todd was giving as good as he got, but Inspector Findlay could only just about manage to hold on to the man twice his size.

Suddenly Todd realised the man he was fighting still held the revolver. It was then the fear struck, and he found a strength he didn't know he had. He grabbed him by the wrist and slammed his arm to the floor while throwing one leg across and pinning him down. Todd pulled his fist back and, with one mighty thud, left the man senseless.

He grabbed the revolver and jumped to his feet. He pointed the gun at the ceiling and pulled the trigger. The ensuing explosion stopped the man Findlay was clinging to for dear life in his tracks.

Todd lowered the weapon and pointed it at him. "Enough!" He shouted, "enough."

All went quiet as Findlay struggled to his feet, "where's Jackson?" gasped Findlay.

Todd pointed to Jackson's desk. "He's hiding over there sir, under his desk."

Findlay grabbed his arm and pulled him to his feet. "Here," said Todd, handing the revolver to him.

"No, no, no, Sergeant, you keep it pointed that way, not this."

Todd pointed to the door. "Move!" he growled.

They made their way back to Torquay police station, with Todd still pointing the gun at them.

That night, Todd and Findlay sat quietly in their office. "I think that's a result sir, don't you?"

"Not really, Sergeant," he said. "Two men are dead, and you nearly made it three. The mill will most likely close down, putting all those people out of work. We could both have been shot, and one thing is even worse than all of this."

"What's that sir?" said Todd.

"When I get home and Mrs Findlay sees the mess my suits in, all hell will let loose!"

Todd just smiled. "Yes sir," he said, "I expect it will!"

THE END

A brief history of Cockington

C ockington is a village near Torquay in the English county of Devon.

The village was founded 2,500 years ago during the Iron Age. There is even evidence of two hill forts on either side of Cockington Village.

Little was known about Cockington from the point up until the remains of a small Saxon village were found near the Drum Inn. The first official documentation of the village was in the 10th century.

Cockington Court (the manor), was owned by Arlic the Saxon, then Robert Fitzmartin. Robert passed it to his son, who renounced the name to become Roger de Cockington. The Cockington family owned the village and estates from 1048 to 1348.

Cockington Manor was sold to the Mallock family in 1654 who owned it until 1932, it was then sold to the local council. Now it hosts art exhibitions, tearooms and weddings.

Cockington Village, possibly one of the most beautiful thatched roof villages in the UK.

Ken Mackenzie

Ken Mackenzie is a bestselling author of many children's books with many talents to his name. Whether it's his long-standing work with the Children's Hospice South West, his beautiful piano playing that transports listeners all around his hometown of Torquay or his children's stories; he takes people on a journey to a brighter, kinder world.

Inspector Findlay is his first mystery novel, inspired by his daily dog walks around the beautiful Cockington Village and grounds of Cockington Court.

Supporting
children's hospice
SOUTH WEST
Registered Charity No. 1003314

Children's Hospice South West provides care for children who have life-limiting conditions and are not expected to live into adulthood, whilst also supporting their whole family. You can find out more about their essential work at https://www.chsw.org.uk

Old Mate Media is delighted to share that 25% of the profits from the sale of Inspector Findlay will be donated to the Children's Hospice to help them continue their essential work.

Also By Ken Mackenzie

Other books by Ken Mackenzie include:

Jasper The Very Lucky Little Kitten

Available from Amazon and in all good bookstores

Gentle George

Available from Amazon and in all good bookstores

Brian The Field Mouse

You can find all Ken's books on Amazon, in Torquay bookstores and directly at Ken's shows.

Turn your book dreams into reality

Do you have a story that you tell your kids and grandkids all the time? Are your friends and family always telling you, "you should be an author"?

Old Mate Media is a specialist publishing company that can help you take your creative thoughts from scribblings to a published book. We walk with authors along the publishing road, stepping in to offer our expertise only where it's needed, so you can create a beautiful and affordable published book.

Visit oldmatemedia.com to find out how we can help you realise your dream.